One Hundred and One Dalmatians

Twin Books

Hi! My name is Pongo. This is my pet, Roger Radcliff. He's a musician. All he needs to keep happy is his piano and his pipe. He's married to his work. But I don't want us to be bachelors forever. It's downright dull. I see no reason why Roger shouldn't have an attractive mate. And that's how this story begins.

3

It was a sunny spring day. The park in front of the house was full of people walking. I was bored, but Roger was too busy with his music to notice that what we needed was a companion. There were lots to choose from. I used to watch them from the window every day. Miss Poodle? No, too snobby, and I was sure Roger would not care for her mistress. That Afghan wasn't too bad, but she looked a bit snooty, and as for her mistress…no, not quite right for Roger.

It's not easy trying to find the other half of a couple. Especially when you're looking for a pair.

5

Ah!!! Now that's better. Look at those two. Perfect! A sleek-looking animal of my own distinguished breed—a Dalmatian. She was so lovely that my heart missed a few beats. And as for her mistress—not bad at all! Tall, elegant, carrying a book—must be a brainy type…just like Roger.

If only Roger could see her. But he's too busy with his music. I can't let those two get away. Quick! I must get Roger's attention.

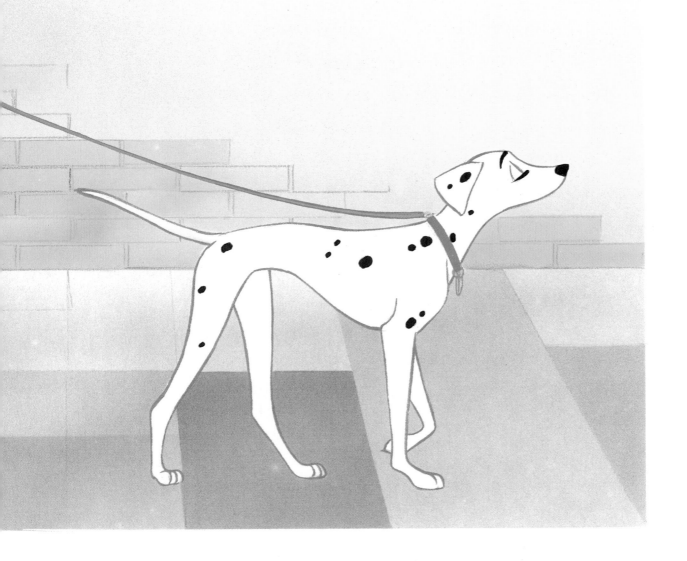

I've got it! I'll just push the clock hand forward with
my paw. When Roger sees the time, he'll take me for my
daily walk.

Clever idea, don't you think? But unfortunately, he's not
looking at the clock. He's too busy tinkering away at the
piano.

Looks like I'll have to make some noise myself.

"WOOFF, WOOFF!" I barked. "Hurry, master, it's time for my walk." I'm not usually so pushy, but this was an emergency.

Roger looked up from the piano. "Time for your walk already? All right, let's go."

There was no time to waste. I grabbed his hat and my leash and carried them to him in my mouth.

I was at the door in a flash, my tail wagging like mad.

10

I spotted them as soon as we entered the park. But Roger decided to sit down beside the pond.

I had to do something. I grabbed Roger's hat and carried it over to the lady.

"WOOFF, WOOFF! Here's a present. It's from that man sitting over there."

Roger wandered over and started to apologize. "He's a silly dog. I'm sorry if he's bothered you."

"Oh, no, really, it's quite all right," she replied.

Sometimes I wonder about these human beings. They are so slow. While they were busy making small talk, the Dalmatian, Perdita, and I had already decided that this was it. We knew that we were meant for each other. We jumped and danced and ran circles around their legs. Soon our leashes became entangled and our humans fell into the pond. Oh, no! This was trouble.

Amazingly enough, though, they weren't even angry. In fact, they laughed. They were soaked from head to toe, but they looked happy. And later...

Well, good old Roger wasn't so slow after all. Before you could blink an eye, he was asking Anita—that's the lady's name—to marry him. Sometimes, I guess, I don't give human beings enough credit.

But it was really Perdita and I who had done all the work. The house became a paradise for dogs and their masters.

14

Our peace was shattered
one day by the simple ring of
the doorbell. Anita answered
the door, with us at her heels.

In walked a creature
wearing a tight satin dress
and fur coat.

"Hello, darling! Remember
me? I'm Cruella De Vil: we
went to school together," she
said, waving her cigarette and
filling the place with smoke.
Phew! It was too much for
my sensitive nose.

She finally came to the
point of her visit. "Anita,
darling, I believe that
Perdita's expecting little ones.
And you know how much I
adore puppies. You will keep
one for me?"

When she left, Perdita and I
looked at Anita. We were
thinking about our puppies.

Anita was thinking about them, too. I don't think she liked the idea of giving one away to that woman, either. When Roger came home and found us all wearing such sad faces, he decided to cheer us up and began dancing with Anita. And before we knew it, we were all dancing and laughing.

Cruella was forgotten—at least for the time being.

The big day arrived. While Anita was helping Perdita, Roger and I waited outside the door. We were both pretty nervous. There seemed to be a lot of noise coming from behind the door. Finally, Anita came out wearing a big smile.

Perdita lay on the cushions with a tired smile on her face. Next to her were five...ten...fifteen little white balls of fluff. Wow! Fifteen puppies! I was the proudest father on the block.

Perdita and I were the happiest parents in the world. Roger even composed a special lullaby for the pups. Things just couldn't have been better.

Riinngg! The doorbell rang so loudly that I jumped into Roger's arms. It was Cruella De Vil. She hadn't forgotten us. "I heard that Perdita and Pongo have fifteen puppies. It's just wonderful news," she cried. She looked down at the puppies. "How much?" she asked, beginning to write out a check. I started to tremble. But Roger was firm. He told her that none of the puppies was for sale.

Cruella got so mad that she splattered ink all over us.

After Cruella stormed out of the house, Roger told Anita that there was nothing to worry about. "She'll never get her hands on our puppies," he said.

As the weeks passed, the puppies' spots began to appear. They were a joy to us. They loved to watch television. Their favorite program was about a dog called Thunder, who was a sheriff's dog in the Wild West.

We used to gather in front of the television every night. Some of the puppies would climb onto the sofa for a better view. Whenever Thunder came on the screen, the puppies would bark with excitement.

One of the little ones, Pepper, stood on my head and growled at the bandit on the screen. Some of the other pups became frightened and ran away to hide under the sofa.

Nanny heard the growling and came into the TV room to investigate. She was the one who looked after us. She helped Anita with the cooking and dusted the piano for Roger. "I think it's time you were all in bed," she said as she began picking up the pups. Good old Nanny!

She put all the puppies to bed in their basket in the kitchen. "Now, now, Penny. Time for you to get some sleep," she gently scolded as she tucked her into bed.

It was time for our evening stroll. As we left the house with Roger and Anita, two men watched us from a truck parked outside the house.

"Okay, there they go. Now it's time to make the move," said one as he saw us walk away.

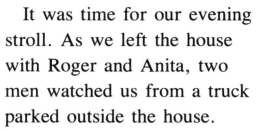

Nanny answered the door.

"Sorry to disturb you, Madam, but we've come about the electricity," said the tall one.

"At this time of night?" Nanny exclaimed. "Come back in the morning. And anyway, there's nothing wrong with the electricity," she said as she began to close the door.

The two men wouldn't take no for an answer. They pushed the door open and went into the house.

"Don't you dare come in here!" shouted Nanny, chasing them into the hall. But they paid no attention.

"Where do you think you're going?" she cried as she grabbed at their coats. The tall one rushed up the stairs, while the other ran toward the kitchen.

"Oh, dear! I wish Master Roger were here," she cried. "What am I to do?"

Soon the two men found
what they were after. It
wasn't money or jewels. They
were stealing the puppies.
The two of them put all
fifteen pups into a big bag.

"Let's get out of here
before the others come
back," said the short one as
they ran out the back door.

Hearing the door slam, Nanny rushed into the kitchen. When she saw the puppies' empty basket, she began to cry.

As soon as Roger heard the terrible news he picked up the phone and called the police. "Our fifteen Dalmatian puppies have been stolen. You must help us get them back," Roger explained to the policeman. "I don't know who could have done this. But please, you must find them for us."

The next morning, Cruella De Vil read of the puppies'
kidnapping in the newpapers. She was grinning from ear
to ear as she picked up the telephone.

"Congratulations, boys. You did a good job. I'll see you
in a little while," she said, and she put down the phone.

In the meantime, Perdita and I decided to take things into our own hands. We would use the twilight bark to send news of the stolen puppies to every dog in London.

The Great Dane and his sidekick, Scottie, were the first to hear the news.

"Who's been kidnapped?" asked Danny, the Great Dane, straining to hear our distant bark.

"I can't believe it," said Scottie. "Fifteen Dalmatian puppies have been stolen. I'll sound the alert."

And the dogs began barking a message that passed from dog to dog all through the city. What a commotion! With all the noise, no one got much sleep that night.

On the other side of the city, Old Towser and his pal, Lucy the goose, picked up the news. "What's that about fifteen puppies?" said Old Towser, who was a bit deaf.

"Someone's stolen Perdita's puppies," Lucy screeched into his ear.

"Well, stop squawking and let's get to work," said old Towser as he ran to the top of the highest hill in the city.

Old Towser sent the message to all the country dogs within sound of his bark.

On a faraway farm, the news finally reached the Colonel, a retired army dog, and his friend, a cat named Sergeant Tibs.

Captain, the horse, was the first to pick up the message. He and Sergeant Tibs woke the Colonel.

"There's an urgent message from London. Listen!" All three perked up their ears.

"Is it war?" asked the Captain, always ready for battle.

"No, it's a kidnapping. Puppies...fifteen Dalmatian puppies...last night," said the Colonel.

Tibs scratched his ear. ''Funny. Last night while I was prowling around the old De Vil mansion, I heard some yelping. The lights were on and smoke was coming from the chimney.''

''Hmm!'' said the Colonel. ''That place has been empty for years. Something fishy is going on over there. Did you say you heard yelping?''

''Sure sounded like dogs to me,'' said Tibs.

''I think this calls for an investigation,'' said the Colonel. ''Come on, Tibs, let's go have a look.''

Tibs jumped on the Colonel's back and off they trudged through the snow. "Look! Pawprints. Lots of them," said the Colonel, sniffing the snow near the deserted mansion.

"And there's a light on—over there in the window," whispered Tibs. Silently, the two crept up around the side of the abandoned building. When they reached the window, they both looked in.

What a scene! In a sofa sat a tough-looking man with a bottle in his hand. Surrounding him were ten, fifteen, twenty, fifty—maybe more—little Dalmatians.

''I thought only fifteen puppies were kidnapped,'' whispered the Colonel.

''That's right. The message said fifteen. What are the rest of these puppies doing here?'' wondered Tibs.

''You go find out what's going on. I'll go back and send a message to Pongo,'' said the Colonel. He headed back to the farm.

Meanwhile, inside the house, all the puppies were gathered in front of the television. They didn't know where they were, nor who the other pups were. But at least there was a TV.

Tibs found a hole in the wall and crept into the room. "This is crazy," he thought. "How am I ever going to tell which of these puppies belong to Perdita and Pongo? They all look alike to me. And there are so many of them. There must be almost a hundred."

"Pssst! You over there. What's going on here?" Tibs whispered into the ear of one of the puppies. The puppy listened as Tibs explained about the kidnapping.

"I don't know any Pongo," said the puppy. "A lady bought me and my brothers in London. We've been here for a couple of days. But some new puppies arrived a few hours ago. There they are in front of the television. I think there were fifteen of them."

Tibs was excited when he heard this. "I must get near the television. But how am I going to get past that man?"

Tibs tiptoed up to the sofa.
Just as he reached the top, the
man moved.

''Maybe if I stay perfectly
still, he won't know I'm
here,'' thought Tibs, as he
froze beside the bottle.

Without looking, the man
reached for the bottle. Instead
he grabbed Tibs by the neck.

"Oh, no! Now I'm in
trouble," thought the cat.

52

Jasper, the kidnapper, didn't realize what he was doing. He was about to take a swig when Tibs let out an enormous "MEEOOWW!!!" Jasper was so stunned that he dropped the cat.

Tibs shot off in a flash.

54

Meanwhile, the Colonel had passed on the news. The message traveled back to the city. Farm dogs told house dogs and so on, until Danny, the Great Dane, heard the word. "The puppies have been found—alive and well," he told Perdita and Pongo.

"Where are they?" asked Perdita.

"They're hidden in the old deserted De Vil mansion."

"So it was Cruella," gasped Perdita.

"Spread the word. We're coming," barked Pongo, as he and Perdita ran off to rescue their pups.

Back at the mansion, Cruella De Vil was busy counting the puppies. She was thinking of all the lovely coats and hats their spotted coats would make.

Seeing Horace and Jasper—the kidnappers—in front of the television, she began to shout. "I'm not paying you to watch TV. Get up, you hoodlums! I want the job done on those puppies before tomorrow."

"Okay! Okay! We'll deal with the puppies as soon as the program's over," said Horace, covering his ears.

Tibs heard everything. "This calls for fast action," he thought. "There's no time to wait for the others to come."

"Quick!" he hissed at the puppies. "Follow me and don't make a sound. You're in danger. I've got to get you out of here—now!"

The puppies were frightened and did as they were told, all except Lucky, who was busy watching television. Neither he nor the kidnappers saw what was happening. Their eyes were glued to the TV.

Tibs had never worked so hard. It was not easy trying
to get all those puppies out without making a sound. Just
as he was pushing the last puppy through the hole, he
heard Lucky barking at the TV.

Rushing back to get him, he saw the program was over.
And Horace and Jasper had realized that the puppies were
gone. They were furious.

At that very moment, Perdita and Pongo were nearing the mansion. They could hear the yelling.

"Hurry," urged Pongo. "Something's going on in there."

Tibs grabbed Lucky and led him off with the others. He
rushed down the staircase looking for a place to hide.
Hundreds of little paws were running as fast as they
could. Some tumbled and fell—but not a cry was heard.

Tibs and the puppies hid under the staircase.
"Shush!" whispered the cat, silencing one of the
puppies with his paw. He heard growling noises. "The
others have finally arrived."

There was a terrible howling and screaming as Pongo and Perdita rushed into the mansion and attacked. They were so quick that Jasper didn't know what hit him. Pongo bared his teeth while Perdita snapped at Jasper's coat. "Leave me alone! I swear I didn't do anything," cried the kidnapper as he fell to the ground.

"Leave this one to me,"
snarled Pongo. "Perdita, you
take care of the fat one."

Horace backed away as Perdita ran toward him. He was trying to reach the fire poker. Patch came to help his mother. The two dogs grabbed the corners of the rug and gave it a yank. *Wooosh! Boom!* Horace fell in front of the fire.

"That will keep him out of our way!" cried Perdita as she, Pongo and Patch ran off to find the other puppies.

Sniff! Sniff! Horace smelled
something burning.
"YOW! OUCH!" he
screamed as he rushed outside,
trailing smoke behind him.

While Perdita and Pongo were dealing with the kidnappers, Tibs led the puppies to the Colonel's farm. And that's where the two parents found them.

The Colonel urged them all to hide in the stable with Captain.

No sooner had the dogs hidden behind a haystack, than
Jasper and Horace appeared. The Colonel watched from
the doorway.

"Look! More prints," said Jasper.

"Yeah! But where are those mutts?" replied Horace,
who was carrying a big club.

"The tracks lead into the stable. Come on. Let's have a
look. They won't get away this time," said Jasper.

The two looked around the stable but found no pups.

"You dope!" cried Horace. "I thought you said they were here."

"Well, I saw the prints. They can't be far away," Jasper replied.

Tibs whispered into the horse's ear. "Okay, Captain, now it's your turn to have some fun. Ready, steady, *GO!*"

Captain struck out with his hind legs. BAAMM! Jasper and Horace went whizzing over the Colonel's head. They landed headfirst in the snow.

Perdita, Pongo and the
puppies slipped out the back
of the stable. They ran with
all their might, but it wasn't
easy for the little ones. Pongo
picked up the smallest one
and carried him in his mouth.

Ahead of them was a farm.
If only they could make it
that far!

A collie came out to meet them. "We'd just about lost hope," he said to Pongo. "We have shelter for you at the dairy farm across the road. You can all rest and get an early start in the morning."

"Oh, thank goodness!" said Pongo, and he turned to Perdita. "This way, Perdy," he said.

All the exhausted Dalmatians turned their noses into the wind and made for the warm barn.

Perdita led the puppies into the barn. Three cows watched them go by. "My, what a big family you have," exclaimed Queenie.

"Poor little darlings. They're tired and hungry," mooed Princess.

"We'll give them fresh, warm milk. That will make them feel better," said Duchess.

When the puppies had lapped up all the milk they could hold, they settled down to sleep.

The Dalmatians were all up and on the run again at dawn.

Perdita and the puppies ran on ahead, while Pongo stayed behind to sweep away their tracks. Soon he heard two cars approaching. It was Cruella De Vil and the two kidnappers.

"This is your last chance, you numbskulls! Follow me into that village. I want those dogs NOW!"

Pongo ran to catch up with his family. Perdita and the pups had met a friendly Labrador retriever who was hiding them in an old coal shed.

"In a few minutes the coal truck will be leaving for London. You can ride in the back," he told Pongo.

At that moment, Cruella drove by. She was furious.

"Look!" whispered Pongo. "She's on our trail. How will we get into the truck without her seeing us?"

"Simple," said the Lab. "Roll yourself in the coal dust. She's looking for dogs with spots, not black dogs."

What a great idea—and it
was fun, too! Pongo was the
first. Then the pups joined in.
Soon they were all black from
head to tail.

Outside there was a sudden screech of brakes. Cruella had found some tracks. She stopped the engine and called out to Jasper and Horace. "Look! Pawprints! They're around here somewhere. Go look behind that coal shed. I'll watch from here. You'd better not botch things up this time—or I'll have *your* skins."

While Cruella was giving her orders, Pongo and the
puppies filed toward the waiting truck. Cruella was a bit
surprised to see so many black puppies. ''I didn't know
they raised Labradors in this village,'' she mumbled as
she watched them go by.

Horace turned to look at the dogs. "Wouldn't it be
funny if Dalmatians turned themselves into Labradors?"
"That would be some miracle," laughed Jasper.
"Stop babbling like fools and go find those dogs!"
screamed Cruella, who was losing her temper.

"What? More Labradors?" she muttered, as Perdita and the last batch of puppies ran past the car. They were almost there…just a few more steps. *SPLAATT!* Some melting snow fell onto Perdita and the pups. Small white spots began to appear on the dogs' backs. Cruella leaned out of the window. Her brain started ticking. "White spots on black dogs…black spots on white dogs. Of course! Those aren't Labradors!"

"You're clever dogs," she said, "but not clever enough. Horace! Jasper! Over here! Those aren't Labradors—they're Dalmatians!"

Cruella De Vil sniggered with delight.

Perdita and the puppies ran for the truck. Pongo was waiting to lift them up, and soon they were all inside. The engine roared as the truck started down the road, just in time! Cruella shook her fist as she saw them drive off. "I'll catch up with them yet! This car of mine can run circles around that old heap."

Cruella stepped on the gas pedal. Her car raced up next to the truck. She was trying to force it off the road, but she didn't see the bridge up ahead. Before she knew it her car had crashed through the railing and was plunging into the ravine.

The car rolled over in the snow several times before
coming to a halt. Parts of the roof and hood had been
lost, but Cruella was still behind the wheel. And she was
madder than ever.

Ranting and raving, she clung to the steering wheel as the car raced back up the hill. Nothing was going to prevent her from having her way. Flames burst from the engine as she sped after the truck.

"Oh, no! Here she comes again!" cried Perdita. "I wish the driver would go faster."

Then Pongo saw the blue van driven by the kidnappers barreling down the hill, heading right for them. But instead of cutting off their truck, Jasper and Horace slammed right into Cruella's car.

BAANNG! CRAASSHH! Cruella and the two kidnappers went flying through the air. The race was over...and Cruella De Vil had lost—forever.

Back in London, Anita was trimming the Christmas tree. It looked like it would be a sad holiday. "Oh, Roger," sighed Anita, "I can't believe Pongo and Perdita would run away."

Nanny entered with some hot chocolate. "Here's a bit of Christmas cheer," she said, "if there's anything to be cheerful about." And she wiped a tear from her eye.

As Nanny started back to the kitchen, she began to hear a faint barking sound. The barks got louder. Suddenly the kitchen door burst open and a pack of black dogs burst in.

Anita backed up against the sofa as one of the big black dogs leaped up on her lap. She put her hands out to fend off the dog, and they came away covered with soot.

"Why, it's Perdita!" she cried, "And all the puppies!"

Soon Nanny and Roger came running into the room.
Tears of happiness streamed down Nanny's face as she
dusted off the little puppies.

"How did they get into this state?" she asked.

"Now that's a real mystery," said Roger. "I suppose
we'll never know. Maybe I can write a song about it."

Perdita and Pongo looked around at their puppies. They
would save their story for their grandchildren.

Anita looked at all the puppies. "There must be a hundred of them!" she said.

"One hundred and one," said Nanny, counting, "including Perdita and Pongo. What a family!"

Everyone was delighted—even Nanny, who was going to have to look after all those puppies.

Roger sat down at the piano. "I *will* write a song," he said, and he began to play. "I'll call it 'Dalmatian Plantation.' "

Produced by
Twin Books,
15 Sherwood Place,
Greenwich, CT 08630

ISBN 1 85469 981 4

Reprinted in 1992

Printed in Hong Kong